A STEP INSIDE

Denis Emorine

Translated from the French
by Phillip John Usher

Červená Barva Press
Somerville, Massachusetts

Červená Barva Press
P.O. Box 440357
W. Somerville, MA 02144-3222

www.cervenabarvapress.com

Bookstore: www.thelostbookshelf.com

Cover Art: "Autoportrait" by Tatiana Samoïlova

Cover Design: William J. Kelle

ISBN: 978-1-950063-03-1

French original "Au chevet des mots"
Publisher : Editions du Gril
11 avenue du Chant d'Oiseaux
1310 La Hulpe – Belgium
Copyright © Editions du Gril, 1998

TABLE OF CONTENTS

PREFACE

Yes, the words themselves are perched at the bedside, reciting only in the captivating, watery language of the subconscious! Here is a collection of vignettes that invites the dreamer into the elusive, entrancing perpetual fever of poetry. Make no mistake, though this is a story of the ineffectual manner of words reflecting meaning, it is the poetry of both Denis Emorine's thoughts and Phillip John Usher's impeccable translation that makes A Step Inside much like simultaneously watching the alluring undulation of an interpretative dancer and an execution. Here you are in the town square of language, where words elope, make love, fight, and part like unsatisfied, restless lovers into the night. It is never enough, it seems, when it comes to language. There are words that masquerade and manipulate, and there is the purity of meaning, as Emorine seems to suggest from the opening quotation used: "And then, we'll be able to talk without stumbling into those words that cause time to bleed."
—Joë Bousquet.

The elusiveness of metaphor, as personified in the first segment, marks you, strangles you, but can never truly be what it is. Metaphor in and of itself can never be exactly what is being said nor can it be what is not being said. Emorine masterfully captures the notion of meaninglessness — the desperation of harnessing meaning from words — all in honest, naked language. Words are without teeth and bones, without structure. And because they can simply be, even in what is perceived by most as a formless state, Emorine is encouraging the simplicity of them in this sensual work. Sensual because there consistently exists a passionate chase between the narrator and his words, any words for that matter. There comes a time when one is reading this brilliant collection, that one realizes that there is no beginning nor is there an end, no divisive lines that separate words and life. Rather — words, language — are just as organic as the body itself, perhaps even eventually serving as a soul transcription. It is the best we can do. Let us visit with the work assuming all the roles: as the words themselves, as the silence, as the narrator, as Franz Kafka even. The heart of this collection is in the segment "Fever", when Emorine declares: "Only silence has the bedside manner needed to respond to words broken down by their plentitude". You may try to stab its "voice face," you may try to escape consonants and vowels from smothering you, you may even try to drink the colors of a rainbow, but there is no remedy to the intriguing ambiguity of words.

Lina Ramona Vitkauskas

And then, we'll be able to talk without stumbling into those words that cause time to bleed.

—Joë Bousquet

A STEP INSIDE

Metaphor

With eyes turned towards the impassive sky, lips biting the wind's gusts, thoughts wondering, I wandered for a long time about the countryside. Uncombed and scruffy, the tall grasses opened their arms towards me, trying to hug me. In vain. Why? I drove them away with a frown, crushed them under foot without a thought. I should have guessed however that nothing is ever written in vain, that innocence exists only on the blank page, and that the smallest sign is first written against oneself.

When I opened the door of the abandoned house, I should have remembered... Lady Death was there, on the threshold, behind me. I turned around abruptly. I should have recalled that "she" is never called upon in vain, that one does not pronounce her name —even as a whisper— without compromising oneself. It was indeed "her". Her green eyes sparkled. Without a blink, we stared at each other in silence. I grabbed her by the throat, beating the air with my arms. She easily slipped away, but I hear her laugh behind my back.

When I came back to consciousness, I was lying on the cobbles. Her breath had quite literally gone to my head. My hair was steeped in that breath. I could easily have remained there on my back, arms crossed on my chest, but no, I got up right away and dusted myself off. I must not broach the question of her name. Not even through the supposed mystery of writing; otherwise, her seal will mark you once and for all. Your life would not be long enough to atone for that moment of abandon.

Obey!

Let the wind shout its pain through the trees. And if, perchance, the hands of the Gods should twist above the treetops, chop them down and show no pity! Do not give in!

The trap

Wanting to strip words of their meaning, I almost fell into my own trap. One night, they got into my room. They attacked me, grabbed me by the throat. They tightened their grasp, harder and harder... I struggled vigorously but I couldn't get my breath. A swarm of letters whirled around me and danced before my crying eyes. Chased by pain, I beat my head against the walls. Finally, a D and an E fell down onto the carpet, only to take flight right away. Consonants and vowels then flew away on the back of a big L. I was saved. For now.

Truth

I am still unaware what others call me. Is that the truth of the dream? Is that what happens under daylight glow? In any case, what does it matter? Sometimes, I play dice to find out the time of my final demise. So far, another hand had always reached out to stop mine, preventing the dice from spitting the bite of a moment right in my face.

When the angry crowd comes requesting a poem, I will open wide my arms, revealing my heart; and they all will be struck down. The ground will open a little to absorb my approval.

The voice

During the night, the voice returned to draw me from sleep. The voice spoke perfect and polished French with a slight Slavic accent. I almost gave myself over. It whispered very low the words I should say, the books I should write, the thoughts that were to guide me. I listened, fascinated. I agreed in silence. It raised me from my bed, led me by the hand towards the sheet of paper that had remained hopelessly blank for weeks. All I had to so, said the voice, was to sit down and take dictation from the voice. You will be given it all, it said. All you have to do is faithfully transcribe each night's silence: let the light stretch out, let the words resound in your most inner self. Then the voice pronounced the name of the woman I love. That was more than I could bear. I took my fountain pen and stabbed it right into the voice's face. A bloody stain covered the paper's whiteness, all of it, drowning the words. The voice disappeared at once. It has never returned.

Since then, I always wake up at the same time, imagining I hear a voice speaking perfect and polished French with a slight Slavic accent. I lend my ear to the night, but I hear only silence. I try to fall back to sleep, but it's impossible. Each night when I wake up, an unexplainable pain invades my face and, on the pillow beside me, I believe I see a red stain growing, growing... ready to drown me.

Nocturnal

At night, I sometimes open the window of my room. My naked body half swallowed by darkness, I look around me, seeking, waiting. The stars hide away the presence of that god who does not exist at these latitudes. I reach out my hand towards the stars, not to grab one, but merely to a gesture at them.

If, by the greatest of chances, one of them answers me, I feign the most total indifference. At once, the star goes out, mortified. Happy to be almost a demiurge, I shut the window, and go back to bed: I have created a miracle that fits me well. The eyelid closes while the breath of night runs slowly between my fingers, wrapping me in mystery.

The book

It was one of those days when the sky leans back on itself ready to launch up still higher; one of those days when birdsong echoes nothing but pure vacuum, when the ground expels man from its meanders, forcing him to take shelter in his home. Alone in the garden, I refused to believe what was so obvious. The hours went by, pointing at me with a disapproving finger.

Darkness filled my head. Submissive, I decided to go back home. The open book awaited me, open to the right page. At once, I took refuge in its arms.

On the Obvious

I always thought I needed very little to live: a pinch of blue on half-open lips, a flower married to a book's curves, the curve fortunately making the path from point to point a little longer... All things considered, all was already traced on the wheat sheaf of silence. All one has to do is to place one's lips on the wheat sheaf, with resolution and free of ideas.

And then the clap of thunder caught up with me. Initially I tried to pretend, to get around it all by taming time. The halter securely fastened—I had to give in to the obvious —is the only judge on the matter.

Fever

Only a few of you had any esteem for me. That's for sure: the river banks around me smelled of corpses. Tears could not bring you back, not really. I tried to clasp you in my arms but you were soon taken over with pain; the pain would rise in you attacking the sleepless nights. You felt awkward at seeing me fly in such a manner, the arms in a cross, above the words.

Know that I hold nothing against you. I got rid of that weapon cushioned by a pillow—too obliging. The nape of my neck, made painful, could no longer support the accusing finger.

Very few of you had any esteem for me.
Only silence has the bedside manner needed to respond to words broken down by their plenitude.

Dawn

Behind the closed door, I spy on the morning scarf that slowly unrolls along the horizon. I do not dare to strike, nor to break in. The words no longer guide me on tiptoes. The dawn leaves me, speechless, on the threshold of the page.

Horizons

Soon, I will spear the rainbow to better melt amongst its colors. I will grab its hair with both hands. The mix of colors will leave me drunk.

All I'll have to do is this: climb out of the window, and let myself be carried by its voice. "Don't drop me!" I will beg with a delicious shiver in my voice. I will take his silence for agreement. Little by little, overcoming my timidity, we will hug and dance, intertwined, the waltz of dupes.

Remedy

hen a thousand suns exploded under my skull, I was busy writing. The pain I felt was transmitted to the page and the writing convulsed. Seizing the page right away, I immediately stuck it to my face. The freshness of this new sensation did me much good. When I took down the aforementioned page, I noticed that it was once again totally blank. The pain had disappeared.

Disobedience

Did I not tell you already? You must not take my books without my permission! You know that! Why did you disobey me? Yesterday, for no reason, you opened one of my bookcases—the one that closes badly—and all my books flew out and away. With a butterfly net, we tried to catch them, but in vain. It is the season for major migrations, true. The books will never return; that is certain. Drunk on their freedom and their unconsciousness, they will be caught by the first pen-pushing hack they meet.

And since then, we've been sleeping in different rooms. No words leave our lips anymore, for they deserted with the books. At night, I sleep badly. I believe I hear them mumbling as I stand in front of the open window. When I approach your window, I distinctly hear sobs but it is not you, I am sure. It is them. It is them who wander in the night without hope of return. In vain I have called them back with the sweetest words I know: no sound leaves my lips. They will never return, it is certain.

Ecce homo

The man in white approached me. His smile was engaging; he wanted to make conversation, but I was wary. I do not know if he realized that. His face carried traces of the magic spell inherent to lies "It is I who commands time" he whispered to me. "This is just one of the strings to my bow. You too could make time do as you wish, impose on time the four winds of your will. Approach, do not be afraid!" I was wary of him: what is the point of mastering time if you don't kill it off? And I closed my eyes. When he returned, his clothing no longer dazzled like before. The glare had faded; the man inside seemed less sure of himself; and I no longer heard his words as clearly "There is no Master of time", I shouted at him "and you! you are certainly not that Master!" His face saddened. His clothing suddenly took on the color of mourning. Abruptly, as he approached me, I understood: I was in front of the large oval mirror of my bedroom into which, with all my force, I launched the tin vase. Far off, through broken glass, I could see the man fleeing towards the forest, covered in blood. I burst out laughing and fell down onto my bed. Let us go! The night will be serene!

Meeting again

Tonight, I was woken by a slight scratching at the window. Initially, in a hurry to fall asleep again, I didn't pay attention. I live on the tenth floor of an old building, it must be a dream. At the moment I closed my eyes again, the scratching began again, in earnest. I opened the shutters and leaned out. It was a dark night, I couldn't distinguish a thing and then, leaning more, I recognized him, with his small suit and black hat: no doubt, it was Franz Kafka! Amazed, I finally managed to speak to him: "What are you doing there, Franz? It is foolish, you will kill yourself!"

As he did not answer, I believed this must be a hallucination caused deep in my unconscious by a recent trip to Prague. But no, he was still there, clinging frantically to the edge of my window. Initially, I thought—I admit it—of forcing him to let go, thus causing him to shoot downwards into the void. After some reflection, I was ashamed of these impure thoughts: one does not act in such a way with death. It would be against the most elementary rules of courtesy. Kafka remained there, sadly, in front of me. I did not know what to do. Motionless, as if suspended in air, he considered me in silence. Suddenly illuminated, I shouted to him:
"Franz, you climbed to the wrong floor! You want the fifth floor. "Why?" he answered, disconcerted.
"Quite simply because both your first and your last name have the same number of letters in them: five!" I said victoriously.
"Thank you, thank you! you have given me some hope" he howled.
And, clutching hold of me, he brought me down towards the ground at a tremendous speed.

Since then, each evening, Kafka and me have been hopelessly striking on the fifth-floor window. But nobody ever opens

for us. However the apartment is inhabited, so I am told, by
an old Czech lady... Milena Jesenskà, I believe her name is.

Face to face

You will not manage to wrestle the words into sentences. This evening, the pressure suffocated you. The dead once again came lurking. They sit opposite you, their sand-filled hourglass in hand. Sand pricks at your closed eyes. In vain you tighten your fists, with great pains time passes through amazed palms. The empty house no longer crosses through the moaning of the days.

The fan

Words fan out wide, flatly placed on the page. I wonder with the tips of my fingers.

Henceforth

When I firmly grabbed the blue stone, I did not suspect my name was written inside it. It exploded right in my face, releasing shards into my eyes of fire.

Now, with no work to be done, I wander on the roads, quick sanded in darkness. Fists and hands reach out towards me but I cannot see them, persuaded that I am the only one to walk in a world taken over by abandonment. The words I have used too often have flown away from my memory. They laugh in my ears, beat wings before my dead eyes, touch my lips with their breath. Plunged in a perpetual night, I have unlearned the taste of time.

I have gathered all my books to make of them a gigantic blaze; but in vain I strike match after match, the fire will not light. I certainly thought of climbing this tower of books but I have always been deprived of any sense of direction. Night is a forest of stubborn signs.

In Solidarity

This time, I could not resist it. When I realized, it was too late: the spider had woven its web on the white page. With the first word, it at once grabbed my pen tip, then what came next, i.e. me! Metaphor had betrayed me. I had always spoken—carelessly— about "webs of words", about the "crawling insects of writing". And here I am now, I have become one of those ants scattered on the page, glued into the dribble of writing! What progress.

At that moment, the other writer sat down at my desk. At first, he hesitated for some time, then I saw his pen-tip advance very slowly towards the paper. All, then, was going to start again. Who ever spoke about writerly solitude as he sits before the blank page? I was free, to some extent. We were to share. When the spider swallowed the point of his pen with remarkable address, I groaned my satisfaction. I was no longer alone: we were finally going to share.

Already, somebody was approaching my desk. I looked at my companion in misfortune, we intermingled our thin black spider-legs with legitimate satisfaction.

That day

The day will come when I will set out without turning back towards this forest of reaching arms. I will not open my eyes, as I will have to guide myself in a geography unknown to men. I will have some regrets at heading off in such a manner, with closed eyes, but other certainties will inhabit my name. The day will come when the nocturnal voices of the sirens will no longer succeed in charming me; I will have changed my opinion about all things. At least, I will endeavor to believe that. It will be too late, dear friends. I will no longer perceive your voices, you will no longer reign unanimously over my life. In my sleepless nights, blood will no longer stream over sheets too white... The past will be a shroud, perforated, that I will savagely exhibit, defending this rag against the plans of the daring ones. I will have a flag no more — did I ever have one anyway, except in my most distant childhood? Admittedly, the smell of wisteria will not have disappeared. I will again easily find the path evaporated in ether. The day will come...

II

FROM MY WINDOW

NOTE

The Mural (Mythologie) excerpt from the French original «
Identités »,short stories, L'Ancrier éditeur ,1994. -Strasbourg

The Virgin and the Shadow (Le Sacre de la Vestale) excerpt
from the French original "Failles",short stories,
Editions Lacombe, 1989. – Paris

Irina excerpt from the French original "De ma fenêtre", short
stories, Simple Edition(www.simpleedition.com)

Twenty- One Hundred Hours (Ce soir vers 21 heures) from
the French Original Encres Vives, 2003 - Colomiers

The Mural

When I ran into my neighbor on the staircase, he seemed unduly surprised at my presence. Perhaps because "ran into" really is the word: I was returning home from school, tired, a heavy head and arms weighed down with assignments to grade; I literally ran into him by mistake, then stammered some banal excuse. He looked at me for a long moment: he seemed to be waiting for someone. I carried on my way.

Once inside my apartment, I took a deep breath, once more cursing my profession
—I'm a Classics teacher—and I tried to set courageously to work...
I had just corrected several assignments, each one more disappointing than the previous—and thus unlikely to get my spirits up—when someone timidly knocked three times on the door.
I could guess who it was: it was him, indeed, awkward and embarrassed, eyes to the ground, not daring to lift his head up. He stood on the threshold, lost.
I curtly told him to come in. I was astonished by his visit: as a new tenant, with a rather wild nature, I had not exchanged three words with this man. What I knew of him was very vague: he was approximately sixty-five years old, a widower already for some time; he was supposed to be a real card. Some claimed he was a painter; others, a sculptor. I really didn't care one way or the other. My only concern was how to get rid of him.

He looked at the table covered with books and papers. His face suddenly lit up. "Ah, someone had mentioned you taught Greek..."
The tone suggested admiration. I responded in an aggravated tone.
"Yes... I teach Greek and Latin and French. I teach all sorts of stuff. So what?"

He did not answer. I thought that my icy answer would dissuade him from continuing the conversation.

"So, you teach Greek..." He shook the head. He was about to open his mouth when I snapped:
"Yes, yes and I have a lot of work!"
He seemed not to understand. He stammered:
"It is you I was waiting for a few moments ago. I surprised you, I believe. Please excuse me."
"Me?" "Yes... "
His face lit up again, transfigured.
"I have a passion for Greece, you know! I used to paint sets for a theater which put on Aeschylus, Sophocles, Euripides... and even Giraudoux... I... I kept some of the props when I left..."
I congratulated him coldly.
"And I thought that you might perhaps be interested in the odds and ends I got hold of..."
He pronounced "odds and ends" with great emotion. "Listen... Another time, I've got other things..." "Are you busy this evening? Your husband..."
"I am divorced... divorced without children. Thus, no urgent housework..." He smiled again.
"Perfect! You can come over to my place, then. That will buck you up."
I hesitated. He seemed like a nice enough guy. I was sorry for having been so abrupt. His sincere admiration, his touching kindness made me ashamed. I silently agreed to go.

I followed him to his apartment. In front of the door, he turned around and pronounced the ritual sentence:
"Don't mind the disorder. You know how bachelors are."
He led me into a room where a whole wall was covered by a fresco. It represented
—in a certain kind of very bad taste—a Greece of the imagination, with an exaggeratedly blue sky, the Acropolis on

28

the right and a landscape of olive-trees and stones, gorged with sun...
"It is beautiful, isn't it? I painted it, three days ago to deal with some issues and catch up on wasted time..."
He sighed and shrugged. "Do you like it, at least?
"Yes, yes, very much so. It is very realistic, you know! ..."
"Really? Oh, that makes me very happy. I have never seen Greece. I almost always paint using engravings or photographs."

He disappeared for a few moments and returned with a used book which he must have used many times. He turned the pages and gave wordy commentary about the illustrations. One of them held his attention particularly. His hand trembled... I leaned over and saw three engravings. Of Athena, Diana and Venus. The reproduction of Venus struck me immediately. My lips outlined a smile: the whimsical engraving showed a

goddess with a generous chest, a light loincloth around her waist! I kept my reflections for myself.

"Three marvelous women, aren't they?" The emotion made his voice tremble.
"Each one marvelous in her own way, of course. They fascinate me so much that..."
He stopped.
"I'm ashamed to admit that..."
My anger had fallen. I encouraged him:
"Continue, please..."
"Well! I can tell you... At the theatre where I worked, I had noticed the costumes of these three divinities, at the bottom of an obscure storeroom... Well... I stole them. They are here, in this apartment! Do you want to see them?"
When all is said and done, I liked this old chap! Never quite met anyone like him; a bit of a nutter. His passion for Greece, even though a little ridiculous, was quite moving.

He returned with two tunics, long, probably Athena's, and another one that was shorter.

"Naturally, I don't have anything for Venus... except a thin piece of fabric as in the engraving... On stage, she appeared covered by a tunic, of course! ...

"She is beautiful, isn't she? what a marvellous body!"

Her face blushed. Her eyes shone. Her timidity had completely disappeared. "I even have Athena's helmet and lance. And also Diana's arc and quiver! ...

He fell silent abruptly. This sudden silence disturbed me. The flame which had animated him seemed extinct. I did not dare to look at him. Suddenly, he began speaking again, this time in a strangled voice.

"It would suit you so well!" "What would?"

"These clothes... the clothes of my goddesses... "

I was disconcerted. I looked at him. He swallowed his saliva with difficulty. I ended up breaking the heavy silence and the malaise created by his last words

"What do you mean?"

He looked me in the eyes. I was astonished by the limpidity of his gaze.

"I mean that the costumes of these divinities would suit you very well: Athena, Diana, Ve..."

He did not dare complete his thought. He blushed. He fixed his gaze on the fresco. I felt awfully awkward. Perhaps he had spoken the way he did out of awkwardness... He raised his head.

"I don't want to waste your time. I... my proposal is serious. I... could you... at least for Athena and Diana?"

All of a sudden, I was afraid.

"But... you are insane! You don't think that..."

"Oh, I understand... You think I'm some kind of pervert!"

He seemed sincerely pained. He insisted awkwardly. "It's not that at all. Will you think it over?"

I felt awkward. My fear had disappeared; still, this proposal seemed so astonishing to me, so strange. I stammered automatically that I would think about it and left.

The following day, somewhat angry, I again met him on the stairs, looking as bewildered as before.

"Did you think about it?" "Think about it?"

"My... proposal. Yesterday..."

I didn't know what to answer: was he going to follow me around every day waiting for an answer? I had answered without thinking the day before, it is true. I reflected: the idea of acting out, of playing a role had something exciting to it... There was no risk involved and ambiguity did not displease me. At length the man's awkwardness convinced me, I said quickly as one jumps in at the deep end.

"I agree"

He started, surprised at my answer:

"Is it true? Is it really true? When?" "Immediately if you want."

"OK. Excellent!"

My heart beat faster as I went into "the Greek room". A bottle of Samos Muscatel and two glasses awaited us. He filled my glass up to the rim.

"Here's to Greece!"

My heart was still racing. A sudden warmth filled me. "My name is Henri "

He passed me the longest of the tunics. Henri avoided looking at me as if he was ashamed. He opened the door of a room.

"Here's the room of... of. "

I entered and closed the door at once. The tunic was silky, soft to the touch. It looked like a nightdress. I stripped off slowly. My heart beat faster as if I were about to play some forbidden game.

I decided to remove all my clothing. It did not suit the goddess with sea-green eyes to keep her underclothing on! I advanced towards the mirror and tied my hair in order to easily slip it under the helmet. Then I opened the door.

Henri silently handed me the lance and the helmet, then moved back a few steps.

Like a child, he clapped:

"Marvelous! Oh, marvelous!"

He was smiling like a kid in a candy store.

Majestically, I sauntered out in front of the scenery, lance in hand. The helmet was a bit tight but no matter. I thought confusedly about my colleagues, my students. Whatever would they have made of seeing me thus dressed up? I stopped and stood

opposite him holding up my lance. He devoured me with his eyes. The goddess lived again, but for him alone…

He was blinking rapidly.

"How about we move on to Diana?"

I hesitated. Was this the magic effect of the Muscatel? Temptation was too strong, it ended up winning.

"OK. Diana."

Henri handed me the next tunic, the arc, the quiver and the arrows. Once in the room, I took off Athena's clothes to dress as the goddess of hunting. Much shorter, the tunic came halfway down my thighs. The cut also meant I was showing cleavage. I hesitated… My heart was beating very fast. There was no time to turn back. I took a look in the mirror and made out the image of a young woman of about thirty years old. Her chest certainly visible under light fabric.

I took the arc, the quiver and some arrows… opened the door… Henri considered me with stupor, fascinated… Extremely moved, I froze on the spot: I was afraid to fall… Finally, I got up the courage, adopting an attitude worthy of the goddess. His eyes were resting on me. I did not feel embarrassed anymore. Neither one nor the other of us moved. We held our breath...

After a few long minutes, Henri spoke, in a voice strangled by emotion.
"Good... you should leave now... Thank you for everything... Until next time, perhaps... "
I nodded "No". Surprised, he considered me without understanding. "What do you mean? No?"
"There is still... Venus..."
His mouth opened, no sound came out. He was amazed. "But... Venus... Look at the book..."
I looked knowing very well what I would see. The goddess was practically naked. A bit of fabric around the waist, hardly hiding her attractive forms... She seemed ready for seduction.
"I know..." I murmured. I smiled and looked him in the eyes. Blood beat in my temples. I was burning up. Fever consumed me. I repeated gently.
"There remains Venus. I want to take on this last role."
Henri answered nothing. His lips trembled. He did not dare to believe that...

The slim bit of fabric in hand, I turned back into the room. I quickly removed Diana's tunic. I was naked... I quickly covered myself with the bit of cloth, quickly and awkwardly. I advanced towards the mirror and contemplated myself for some time. Yes, I was Venus, she who incarnated love. I waited still... I must get my entrance exactly right. The light of the bedside lamp accentuated the transparency of the fabric. I decided to place this lamp behind me: the effect would be irresistible. I looked at myself one last time, the bare breasts, the untied hair sweeping down my shoulders... The thin bit of fabric around my waste, sitting very high on my thighs, I liked myself infinitely. School was miles away. Venus was going to be offered to her admirers...

I opened the door slowly, very slowly. At once Henri turned his head in my direction, his avid hands trembled, he opened his eyes wide, filled with wonder by the appearance of the goddess... I advanced, he looking at me, agog... As I moved, the bit of fabric untied itself and fell to my feet. His gaze penetrated me... He too advanced slowly, very slowly. His hands moved irrepressibly. I stood still. I did not even try to pick up the indecent bit of fabric. His hand lightly touched my breasts and I closed my eyes...

Irina

To Sao Iovleff

He was fifty-six. For a little over a year the attacks had become less frequent. In the bedroom mirror he saw a puffy face with thickened traits. Jean had never found himself handsome but, recently, he had been avoiding his reflection in the mirror. He sighed, turned around. The writer, as Jean called himself, looked down at his watch: she would be here soon. The young woman had come up to him yesterday, after the conference, and said she was a journalist. She wrote for some review whose name he didn't know. What was her name again? Irina... Curious, he thought, a Russian first name and yet she spoke

with an Italian accent. The writer, who loved things exotic, was delighted by this unexpected contradiction. Irina had wanted to continue the interview in a more private setting. "My hotel room, is it really suitable for me to meet a young woman there who could be my daughter?" thought the writer smugly, proud of himself. Right away, he had made his advances with a disconcerting amount of self-control. And beautiful Irina hasn't tried to push him away: "What will be will be" she replied, her eyes lighted by a will for challenge.
Jean had seen her walk away, unsettlingly striking in her suit of royal blue. Irina waved a small wave before disappearing. "This evening, she would be his, that was sure." Back at his hotel, a message was waiting for him from the mysterious journalist which left no doubt as to her intentions. The writer was gloated on his luck. Decidedly, literature could lead to anything or rather... to anyone, he corrected, happy with his stroke of   wit.
Jean thought about his wife who had stayed in Paris and he quickly realized -not displeased- that he was going to cheat on her for the first time. For sure, there had been plenty of opportunities but, in thirty years of marriage, the writer had

only committed adultery in his imagination. So, why then take this opportunity at a conference in Lisbon on "Culture : Europe's (heavy) conscience"? He didn't know. Their meeting certainly had spice to it. Obviously, literature was only a pretext: the unknown woman was no more a journalist than he was an archbishop; she had deliberately chosen to seduce him. It was not an unpleasant thing. He flicked through Pavel Armoria's "Trajectories", one of the books he'd taken with him: "The room was in darkness. At present, the old man had nothing to wait for. He opened his eyes... Rain covered the town." This sentence made him somewhat melancholy. The coincidence struck him: it had been raining over Lisbon since he arrived. What did that matter? He was going to roll in the hay with this belle inconnue! No call for the blues, huh? "It's the first time", he thought again. "Another good reason to make the most of it, at your age added an interior voice. She would soon be here now. Jean imagined Irina, slowly undressing in front of him, revealing... All of a sudden, his heart was knotted with pain: quickly, my medication, quickly! Had he at least brought it with him? Bent in two, panting, he rummaged in his suitcase... Not there! Where had his wife put them? ... Yes, he remembered now, his pills were in his suit, on the bed! While he dragged himself towards the crumpled clothes, someone knocked at the door. He didn't open. Irina was in front of him. She looked at him with an indescribable expression. "Is this what you're looking for, oh love of my life?" she laughed. Jean looked up. His medication! How had she been able to... She must have taken it from his pocket while they'd been speaking. The writer winced with pain, it was a serious attack. Irina was a couple of steps away, her poise a challenge. She took off her long blue dress, she was naked. "Come get them if you want them, my love", she murmured, "but you'll have to tackle me and my body. Be careful, the doctor's told you to avoid strong emotions". Jean could no longer offer any reply. The pain was increasing, his breath was short. "One last time..." he mumbled. All of a sudden, he had the impression his wife

36

was leaning over him, placing her hands on his shoulders. Jean felt a kind of well-being wash over him. He reached out his arms in her direction, tried once more to stand up before crashing down heavily to the floor.

The Virgin and the Shadow

That evening when he called me up, he told me in a frightened voice, full of anxiety, that we had to meet up. It was important, vital even that we do so.

While talking he would stop all of a sudden and let the conversation break off; I could feel how defenseless he was, he was tormented and increasingly distressed.

I ended up inviting him over to my place when he reticently warned me that he could not go into any more detail on such a delicate topic.

While waiting for him to arrive, I kept on wondering about this unexpected turn of events: I had known G... for three years. At first, we had met up quite regularly. Eighteen months later, we were meeting up less and less often, rarely even. I couldn't understand why, all of a sudden, he wanted us to meet up. Why this need for silence that made him hesitate as he spoke these sentences that had obviously been carefully prepared? Three years ago, he had been such an orator. I wondered what other changes were afoot for him, and for me...

*

The doorbell rang, shrill, almost prying; it put an end to my confused thoughts. He was here. Physically, he hadn't changed: slim, straight brown but messy hair of

which a lock reached down and divided up his high forehead, falling all the way down to his glasses which rarely moved from the very end of his nose.

We were directly opposite each other, awkward, in an uneasy silence; we didn't dare look each other in the eyes. In a hand that -I think- was shaking, he took my hand and squeezed it gently.

"So, this is where you live..." The blandness of his remarks was probably intentional, an effort to open up communication. He was obviously waiting for me to open fire, but waiting is one of the things I do best: I can -when circumstances so require it of me- hide my impatience behind a mask and remain completely unruffled.

I gazed at him as a cat stares at a mouse. I had the upper hand. How could someone who used to be so relaxed in conversation shut himself up in this monkish silence?

He gave in, and he started to look at me, looking at me who was looking at him; his eyes followed mine.

"For a while now, a strange and penetrating dream..." he started, alluding to his favorite poet Paul Verlaine. He was still a big reader of French literature, I could see. "...has turned into an obsession, and imprisons me inside myself. Or maybe I shut myself inside the dream, I don't know. This dream directly concerns you, directly; you are implicated in the dream..."

There it was, the attack had happened. I had been expecting it, I knew he wouldn't stay trampled down for long in his defeated and imploring attitude. He was now more relaxed and started walking around the room; although still somewhat awkward, he was starting to speak with his former confidence. G... was becoming the person I'd known before, his magnetism was coming back, a magnetism due to his quiet and justified projection of his intellectual superiority that he would parade around when striking poses.

Once again I was carried gently along by his well-constructed sentences, as articulate as they were intelligent. Didn't he always say: "You can't be articulate without being smart! The question, then, is whether to speak like a fool or a wise man!". His speech was as well-oiled as the first days I had known him. All of a sudden, he fell silent, as if he felt awkward. A revelation, the reason for his visit, made him short of breath: "It's something quite unexpected; every time I dream, I see myself giving a kind of show in front of you, and you're the only witness to it, silent and approving."

I heard the creaking again. Snap. I looked at him kindly, encouraging him to carry on.

"It's a kind of revelation... Yes, that's what it is, for I keep making revelations to you, again and again, and each time it's the same place, in this apartment..."

I couldn't understand, or maybe I was too afraid to understand. Eventually, he ended up putting the cord around his neck: "Perhaps you'd understand this better if I were a woman... Moreover, you have to take into account moral, intellectual (and thus social) prejudices."

1 Allusion to a famous poem by Paul Verlaine which begins : "Je fais souvent ce rêve étrange et pénétrant / D'une femme inconnue, et que j'aime, et qui m'aime / Et qui n'est, chaque fois, ni tout à fait la même / Ni tout à fait une autre, et m'aime et me comprend." In English: "I often have this strange and penetrating dream / of an unknown woman, that I love, and who loves me / And who, each time I dream, is never exactly the same / Nor completely different, and who loves and understands me."

The door was ajar and opening further onto the truth contained within, onto what might even be called his obsession, but I wanted him to admit it outright, even if I have to provoke him with some subtle game of questions and answers neatly woven together.

"So, I'm the spectator?"

"Yes, you're watching a play, my play, which I've planned right up to the smallest details, including the decor and the costumes..."

He stopped again, confusion on the edge of his lips and covering his cheeks. G... had stumbled over the pronunciation of the word "costumes", as if this term had walked him too close to some personal system of references which now loaded him with guilt.

I wasn't sure what to do, but decided to finish: "So, let's get to the conclusion."

Then, clearly, articulating each syllable, he admitted his dream to me: "I often dream, then, that I'm getting undressed in front of you; it is possible that this physical stripping hides or symbolizes the need for some deeper revelation, but I'm sure that I need to satisfy this desire to be rid of it and reassured." He was becoming more verbose. "I'm not trying to explain the reasons for this desire; but I need to satisfy it..."

"Would you accept... ?"

How could I not have accepted? I was, I admit, somewhat intrigued, curious even to attend this "theater play" that was more like a cabaret striptease than anything else, or at least that is how it seemed.

My heart was beating at quite a pace. I let G... direct the scene, chose the setting, organize the elements of the decor.

All of a sudden, he stared at me again:

"We need some background music." "Do I get to chose?" "Yes."

I thought about it... Sensual, light music, something unreal would certainly be suitable.

"Jeux and the Prelude to Après-midi d'un faune by Debussy." "Fine."

I settled myself down into an armchair, the only one in my whole apartment. I felt like I was at the theater, waiting for the next act.

The music surprised me, shook me out of my thoughts. I let myself be carried along by Debussy's graceful arabesques. I was tempted to shut my eyes, but the show was also visual.

He turned towards me: "Make yourself as absent as possible; I don't want to hear or see you, I just want to know that you're somehow present."

Following this last piece of advice, I kept quiet though I remained anxious. He took off his jacket, his pullover, his movements followed on smoothly from each other, gracious, airy, in an unexpected choreography.

Finally, I saw his torso, his shirt slipping over white smooth skin that reflected the spot-light shining down on him.

His gestures became more definite, his hands slid over his body, sometimes gently brushing it; he turned around on the spot very slowly, offering this body to my attentive being. His skin played with the light in a game of shadows and moving reflections, strange, surreal, like accomplices to each other.

Very slowly he removed his trousers, turning around to face me. At certain moments, G... would shut his eyes in ecstasy. His clothes, like dead leaves, silent, fell off, or rather piled up, dried up and became inanimate as soon as they were no longer twirling around his body.

G... was now wearing just his briefs, he was rocking slightly, first with his back to me, then facing me, gently touching his thighs, his buttocks, his lower abdomen, pretending to take off that which stopped his revelation from being complete.

Then his briefs slightly revealed his buttocks, just the top of his buttocks, or rather the curve of the small of his back. His hands seemed to hesitate, climbed again to the base of his neck, towards his shoulders that he caressed before going down again to his hips. The briefs fell a little lower.

The music unfurled in convolutions suddenly loaded with significant meaning.

G... illustrated it by giving to the music its sacred and sensual function.

His hands crept between the forms hidden by the unwelcome piece of cloth which would eventually have to disappear. The bulging skin was becoming clearer, surrounded by his nudity that was increasing little by little as the protective envelope was opening.

All of a sudden, his buttocks popped out, very white, exaggeratedly curved and saturated by the light, dazzling with light.

He directed them towards me, gently bent forward, then slowly turned around on the spot. His gestures which had appeared to be hesitant, started to become more definite, and were making him look like the master of his craft.

A kind of black moss appeared a couple of inches below his bellybutton, who knows how it had washed up on this rock that was his body? It seemed to grow with each breath, with each movement. I couldn't take my eyes off it, it fascinated me. He was in front of me, his skin trembling, his briefs, slightly lowered, were molded around his lower abdomen. G... spread his legs, arched his back in order to give to his movements their full power, and to emphasize a nascent secret, dark, lost in mystery and shadow.

The form of his member was more or less clear depending on his mobile and capricious bending movements; he was showing more and more of this intimate receptacle. The black shadow, curly, was growing, undulating, independent of the whiteness that surrounded it, that interrogated it.

Finally, little by little, in small movements, almost as if oiled, his briefs fell down, were set free from his crotch and his thighs and, when this Adonis finally revealed his member, when it was finally in the open, free, offered up to me, directed by the light, when he opened his legs while bending backwards, his arms and the tips of his fingers reaching to the floor, ready to take off for a supreme flight, I realized that I wanted him.

Twenty-One Hundred Hours

To Ilona W.

A few years ago, I was invited to a poetry festival, taking place in S---, a small city in northern Romania, not far from the Hungarian border. (This small detail has its importance.) There were writers of several nationalities, mainly from Eastern Europe, and a few from Western Europe, including a handful of completely uninteresting fellow- French writers. For my part, I spent my time with Romanian friends, in particular with Vasile, the director of an important publishing house in Bucharest, Oglinda.

And then there was Marika...

Moreover, it was thanks to Vasile that I had been invited to this gathering in the first place. He has been translating my poems and short stories for Romanian reviews and was planning to publish an anthology of my texts for Oglinda. I had met Vasile in 1996 in Iasi. We immediately struck up a friendship. Like many of his compatriots, he spoke French remarkably well. An excellent writer of poetry and prose, he often also wrote in French, which he would then translate into Romanian and vice versa. Vasile had also translated many French-speaking writers for various Romanian publishers.

I arrived at the Bucharest airport in early evening. Vasile and his wife Ioana had come to pick me up. Ioana had driven all the night in order to arrive by early morning.

Having left my luggage in the hotel room and quickly freshened up, I joined the other participants somewhat tired and understandably excited. The debate started: "What is the place of poetry in contemporary society?" Each one of us, including me, had something to say on this vast subject. Everyone spoke their own language, plus there was simultaneous translation.

We ate our meals together. The expenses of the stay were taken care of by an international banking organization, famous for its generosity (!). Certain writers were having fun stuffing their faces like nobody's business. "My goodness, Eastern Europeans are famished, it is well known," I said to myself, "it is thus completely excusable." The first day, at lunch, an Estonian had collapsed, dead-drunk, in the restaurant and was discreetly evacuated to the nearest hospital. Vasile leaned towards me: "You now see where poetry is in contemporary society? On the floor! What a fine symbol!"

The conference, debates, and poetry readings were to start up again around 4 p.m. In the meantime, we all spent our time as we pleased: unending discussions, prolonged drinking sessions, a nap, or both. While Ioana recuperated from the fatigue of the voyage: driving her old Renault 14 (which, kilometer by kilometer, got closer to giving up the

ghost) was a real exploit! On the coastal roads especially, the engine, out of breath, huffed and puffed...Vasile and I had decided to go for a stroll, with no precise destination in mind. Rather affluent, at least seemingly, S--- was very much like any town in Western Europe, a fact my friend pointed out to me.

Around the main town square, the prostitutes—no, I will not say "whores", I hate that word—were looking out for prospective customers. "Just right for tea-time" said Vasile with a sense of humor that, for once, I did not appreciate. We were talking, in French naturally, since my knowledge of Romanian is limited to a handful of words (some of which are not that polite !). Vasile explained how one of his manuscripts, confiscated under the dictatorship, had been miraculously found in the files of the Securitate. It was a violent critique of an imaginary totalitarian régime in the form of a parabola by which the censors had not been deceived: "Razbunarea calicilor" ("The Revenge of the Paupers"). It had just been published after more than twenty years and had been warmly received by Romanian critics and billed as the novel of a whole generation. Vasile felt like he was rediscovering a youth confiscated by the dictatorship; making it a somewhat bitter rediscovery. His novel was going to be published in Russia, translated by our friend, the poet Alexandre Karvovski. We planned to translate it into French together.

All of a sudden, a young woman, not much more than a girl, approached us asking "Voulez-vous passer la nuit avec moi ?" More than the question in French, it was the extreme reserve of her speech which surprised me. Taken by surprise, Vasile answered her in Romanian with a brusque tone. I, in French, said "Excuse me?". She repeated, still in French, "Would you like to spend the night in my company?" I looked at her more attentively. She seemed to be about twenty, or maybe slightly older. Not really knowing what to do or rather what to say, I heard myself answer: "No, thank you".

She laughed: "Typical French politeness!"

I was a little embarrassed, I must say. Vasile was being humorous: "Come on, we'll be late!" Noting how uneager I was to move on, he added: "If you want a quickie, it's up to you, you can catch up with her this evening! It can wait for now, can't it?".

We moved on, me with regret, while the girl recited the beginning of a poem by Verlaine, staring right at me. I turned my head in her direction, and stood still while Vasile was still trying to drag me along. In a blank voice, I stammered that I would come back later. He glanced at me with no illusions, lacking all amenity, groaning something in Romanian, before going off. I raised my eyes. She was still there, looking at me attentively. I took a few steps in her direction. She smiled at me, murmuring: "Sous le pont Mirabeau coule la Seine/ et nos amours faut-il qu'il m'en souvienne?" We were alone. Or, rather, I pretended not to notice the other women all wearing lots of make up and too vulgar for my taste. "Je m'appelle Marika..." she told me, smiling. I didn't say a word. She had brown hair, with soft locks falling down to her shoulders. She was slender, beautiful. I felt ill at ease. Marika kept smiling. "I

46

don't have too much time" I managed to articulate. I must get back to the others..." I took a few steps, turned around: she hadn't moved: "This evening, perhaps?" I said quickly. "Around 9 o'clock?"

Marika laughed: "Isn't it more correct in French to say twenty-one hundred hours?" She was right. I said so and then left quickly without looking back.

I arrived late, of course, to the reading. A seat was still free near Vasile. I pretended not to see it, taking instead a seat in the last row next to a Macedonian who looked at me curiously. I asked him in English whether the debates had been going on again for a long time. He laughed and said yes. The poets were about to read some of their work, he added. I couldn't concentrate on listening to the poems. I thought of... I closed my eyes for a moment. My Macedonian neighbor poked me, bringing me back to reality: "Hey, it's your turn!" How did he know my name? That's right, I'd forgotten we were all wearing badges with our name and nationality. I had just been called.

Unsure of myself, I moved towards the platform... I approached the microphone...

I would have liked so much for her to be there in the room...

Around nine o'clock, or rather twenty-one hundred hours, I had succeeded in stealing away form my hosts, interrupting an improvised debate during dinner on "the writer's bad conscience." Did I have a bad conscience? As a writer or as a man? Difficult to say... Both, perhaps... Vasile was in some kind of mood with me, more or less. To tell the truth, I could not blame him for his attitude. During the previous week, he had organized on my behalf appointments with publishers, a debate on contemporary French literature with French teachers and students in the arts centre of S--- and I had kept on avoiding him.

I walked quickly in the direction of the infamous square. Several women were milling about in the fresh September air.

None sought to retain me. Finally, I caught a glimpse of Marika. My heart skipped a beat. She rushed towards me, grabbed my hand tightly : "I was sure you'd come!" she said simply. I was grateful she didn't come up to me like to any other customer...

She took me by the hand. Simply and gracefully. I looked at her. Marika was still dressed in black, amber-colored eyes, gracious, fragile and strong all at the same time. I know, it all sounds banal but I can do nothing about it since that's the truth. We climbed a rather steep staircase. "Here we are" she said, opening the door of a tiny apartment. Its musty smell suffocated me. A simple folding bedstead filled up almost the whole room. I felt oppressed. The window was open wide. "I try however to let as much air in as possible," Marika tells me as if excusing herself, "but..."

She stayed opposite me. I felt terribly awkward. Was it the difference in age? A 47 year old man and a girl of twenty? Not really... but could I explain to her. Marika approached me. We were both intimidated. "Do you want...?" she began... I gestured a "No". She did not seem surprised by the attitude of this rather disconcerting customer.
"I came to talk." I murmured, "...with you. I don't want to... to..."
"...to sleep with me?" she said while smiling
"Yes... or rather, no. "I said sitting on the bed. She sat down next to me.

We spoke for a long time. She was Hungarian, a student in French. A part-time prostitute to help pay for her studies since her parents, having only just enough to live on, did not have the money to "support" their eldest daughter through her studies. Marika was writing a thesis on French poets of the early 20th century. At which university? In Hungary? In Romania? She did not wish to reveal such details. I did not insist. Having

learned that a poetry festival was going to taken place in S---,
she had made her way there, had borrowed this poor wretch
of a room from a friend in order to better "devote herself to
this food-earning occupation"—her own terms.

"When I heard you speak French with your Romanian friend,
I could not resist. I accosted you..."

Time was passing. We were still speaking. An insane idea
crossed my mind: Marika could perhaps speak at the poetry
festival, I could present her... In a ridiculous moment, I
suggested it to her. She nodded "No". Of course, she was
right. Another, even more insane, idea seized hold of me: I
should bring her back to France where she could finish her
studies in peace, but I did not dare suggest it to her.

I rose to leave, suggesting that we meet up the following day,
perhaps a little earlier. "No, not tomorrow," she says,
"because..." I diverted my eyes. She was already "taken," I
thought. "Taken"—what a horrible word, really! I tightened
my hand on her. She tightened her grip without saying a
word.

"The day after tomorrow, then?" "Right, then. The day after
tomorrow."

I left quickly without looking back. Once outside, I shivered.
This feeling did me good. I stretched a little. I was numb. I
raised my eyes. The night was beautiful, my first night in the
company of Marika... I hastened my step. I was in a hurry to
return to the hotel. The streets were deserted. What time
could it be? I had no idea: I was both shaken and happy at the
same time. "You are completely insane," I said to myself.
"You will never change!" As if to prove myself right, a cat
meowed sadly, close by. I would have liked to have stroked it,
but it remained hidden.

"So, it's all going well with the whore? "Vasile asked the next
morning. I didn't answer. Actually, I wanted to slap him! but
how could I be upset with him? Appearances were against
me. I suddenly decided to phone my wife in Paris.

"How are you?" she asked. "You sound strange."

I affirmed in vain that the travel and the long car trip had tired me out. She was not easily deceived.

"Don't worry, I'm fine! It's just that I've felt a little strange since I arrived." I soon hung up, after having asked about the children.

The day went by. Unrelentingly. However, in the arts centre with the other French writers, I had temporarily forgotten Marika. Vasile had introduced me cordially to the audience. I read some short stories. The students' questions were interesting. I will not see her today, I thought to myself... I decided to present my excuses to Vasile who had done so much, but how could I explain the real situation? Vasile willingly accepted my excuses, nevertheless informing me that the Romanian editors were not at my orders, and that it was up to me to set up another meeting as soon as possible. I agreed. My friend looked at me curiously. We had known each other for a long time, but I could not see a way of revealing the situation to him: Marika interested me as someone to talk to, not as... Not believing me, Vasile would probably laugh and then tell me, using one of the typically French expressions he relished in, that "he would not set the bomb ablaze and that I was in any case a big boy..."

The following day, of course, I saw Marika again, and the day after that... My stay was getting close to its end. I would have liked to... What would I have liked, exactly? To prolong my stay? To no longer meet up with her each evening around "21 hundred hours"? To break up, if one can use such an ambiguous word... or quite simply to announce in a light-hearted tone to my family: "Here, let me introduce you to Marika. She is a student of French, and a prostitute in her spare time to pay for her studies. She will be living with us"? But, it is a well-known fact, the human being is generally weak. Undoubtedly, I would not make any departures from that rule.

It was the eve of my departure. That evening, she was not "taken" or, perhaps, she'd freed up her schedule to see me. I arrived a little early at the infamous square where I could no longer feel the evening freshness. As if they'd agreed on it, none of the prostitutes paid any attention to me. And I reciprocated, ignoring them. All dressed in black... they wandered about in silence. To what was this unusual garb due? Vaguely nauseated by the smell of cheap perfume, too strong and heady for my taste, I wandered about in the middle of a strange female ballet, which evoked for me Death's dance, roaming in search of approving victims. My throat was dry. My student ran towards me, her hand stretched out. She seemed delighted to see me. I kept her hand in mine, perhaps a little too long.

"How about we grab a bite to eat?," I suggested. Marika shook her head.

"No, I have plenty of food in my small room." I did not insist.

"I leave tomorrow," I said quickly.

She did not answer, turned her head towards me, smiling.

"Demain, dès l'aube, à l'heure où blanchit la campagne, je partirai. Vois-tu, je sais que tu m'attends."

I stopped her with a gesture.

"Do you have a poem ready for each circumstance of life?" Her disarming smile made my heart wince.

Her room was still just as tiny. We sat on a small corner of the bed, as usual. We both had trouble finding words. With my head lowered, obstinately staring at the ground covered with a fitted carpet which must have been blue, I started to think... Marika wore a red scarf over her ever-present black dress. The gift of a customer? A symbol I didn't understand? She turned to me, gently took it off and handed it to me.

"It's for your," she said finally. I took her hand.

"I will not forget..." I started.

"You must not say that... You mustn't... You should leave now." "Are you chasing me out?"

"No, but saying goodbye is always difficult and... we will never see each other again."

I remained silent. And all of a sudden, I spoke.
"Marika, I can leave you my address... or if you give me yours, I can send you

books for your studies..."
Her face was close to mine. Her eyes looked into mine. Amber eyes. She spoke a few words in an unknown language... Hungarian? I don't know. The room was half in

shadow, and me too. Marika's hands slipped into mine. She rested her head on my shoulder. Very gently. I did not move. Time had stopped. I wanted to remain there forever. Who ever would find us like that? Death?

Moartea, moartea mereu... în oglinzi
opaca
Cu gratii de sînge...

These few worms of Vasile returned slowly to my memory... I had brought my last novel to Marika. She clapped her hands like a child. To make me, rather us, feel more at ease, I tried to summarize the story.
"It's about a man whose wife has just died. He was Russian. Insane with sorrow, he leaves for Moscow and decides to research his late wife's origins, to look for traces of her family. He wanders hopelessly along streets and around cemeteries, he sleeps anywhere he can, questions people in order to give life to her memory. Everyone thinks he's insane..."
I stopped. It was ridiculous. I could feel Marika's breath on my cheek, on my lips...

"You should leave now. Otherwise, we'll perhaps do something crazy."
Why is it now difficult for me to distinguish her face? Tiredness, of course,

eternal tiredness! Why do we always hide the truth from ourselves? Why? It was too late to ask such questions. I knew the answer too well. The human being is weak... Why would I have made any departures from that rule?
I stood up, awkwardly. Marika followed me out. I took refuge in her arms, my face hidden in her hair. She said a few words in Hungarian...

***

Today, I received a letter from Vasile. I've been invited to S---- in Romania, very close to the Hungarian border.
"There will be many writers. I'm absolutely counting on you coming," he wrote. "You're going to receive a great poetry prize (I should not be telling you) and, on this occasion, I will publish an anthology of your texts in a bilingual French/Romanian edition. Ah, and I was forgetting... a Hungarian editor contacted me recently. He's going to write to you: he wishes very much to publish your last book..."

"Death, always death... / in the opaque / mirrors / with their bars of blood."

ABOUT THE AUTHOR

Denis Emorine is a French writer. He was born in 1956 in Paris. He has an emotional attachment to English because his mother was an English teacher. He is of Russian ancestry on his father's side. Writing, for Emorine, is a way of harnessing time in its incessant flight. Themes that re-occur throughout his writing include the Doppelgänger, lost or shattered identity, and mythical Venice (a place that truly fascinates him). He also has a great interest for Eastern Europe.

His theatrical output has been staged in France, Canada (Quebec) and Russia. Many of his books (short stories, plays, poetry) have been published in Greece, Hungary, Romania, South Africa, and the United States.

His first novel *La mort en berne*, 5 Sens éditions, was published in Switzerland, in 2017.

An English translation *Death at Half-Mast* is available in the USA

https://www.experimentalfiction.com/

In 2015, Denis Emorine was awarded the Naji Naaman Literary Prize Lebanon (honor prize for complete work)

For more information, visit his website at:

http://denis.emorine.free.fr/ul/english/accueil.htm

ABOUT THE TRANSLATOR

Phillip John Usher is Assistant Professor of French and Comparative Literature. His book *Errance et cohérence: essai sur la littérature transfrontalière à la Renaissance* (Paris: Classiques Garnier, 2010) deals with the topic of Renaissance border-crossing and globalization. As a translator, he is the author of the first English-language version of Ronsard's epic *La Franciade* (1572) (New York: AMS Press, 2010) and of Denis Emorine's *No through world* (Edmonds, WA: Ravenna Press, 2004). He has also translated various academic and non-academic articles and works. His articles have appeared or are forthcoming in the *Bibliothèque d'Humanisme et Renaissance, La*

Revue des Amis de Ronsard, L'Esprit Créateur, French Forum, and elsewhere. Educated at the University of London (UK) and Harvard University (Cambridge, MA), he regularly lectures in the United States and Europe and has held a visiting position at Boston University (fall 2009). He regularly organizes lectures in the "Translation Across the Disciplines" series and is the webmaster for the Barnard Center of Translation Studies.

BOOKS BY DENIS EMORINE

Plays

On The Platform, (Cervena Barva Press, 2008)
Passions, (Cervena Barva Press,2010)
Closing Time, (JAC Publishing & Promotions, 2011)
The Mistake, (JAC Publishing & Promotions, 2012)
After The Battle, (Big Dog Publishing, 2013)
The Visit, (Off The Walls Plays, South Africa, 2013)

Poetry

No Through World, (Ravenna Press, 2002)
Side by Side, (Foothills Publishing, 2006)
Letters to Saïda, (Cervena Barva Press, 2011)
Poems to Recite While Waiting For War, (Oliver James Press, 2012)

Anthologies

In the Arms of Words, Poems for Disaster Relief, (Foothills Publishing, 2005)
In the Arms of Words, Poems for Disaster Relief (Sherman Asher Publishing, 2006)
Butterfly away, (Magnapoets, Canada, 2001)
Strangers at Home, (Numina Press, 2008)
World Poetry Year Book, (The Earth Culture Press, China, 2014 and 2015)

CD
Attoho 1 (JEF Books, Journal of Experimental Fiction)

www.ingramcontent.com/pod-product-compliance
Lightning Source LLC
Chambersburg PA
CBHW030530260626
47157CB00005B/1955